1

The Senga Series

Senga and the Loch Ness Monster

Senga's Continued Adventures in Scotland

Senga and the Scottish Unicorn

Senga and the Scottish Unicorn

Roslynne McHutchon Mayer

Contents

Chapter One

St Augustine, Florida.

It was the last day of school before the summer vacation. Senga's class was visiting an old fort, "Castillo de San Marco," in St Augustine, Florida. One of the oldest standing structures in North America. Two of her best friends, Piper and Emmerson were with her.

Senga was listening to their guide very intently. She loved history, and she was learning a lot. She found out that the name "Florida" came from the Spanish word, "La Florida," meaning "full of flowers." She was amazed to hear that the fort was built with "Coquina," the Spanish name for 'tiny shells.'

"Who would have thought that a building made of shells could still be standing proudly over 300 years later?" the guide went on to say. "Spain ruled Florida as a colony hundreds of years ago. The explorer Juan Menendez de Aviles founded St Augustine in 1565. For the first one hundred years, St Augustine had many pirate attacks. After English pirates attacked and looted the town and made plans to return to seize St Augustine for their own, Queen Regent Mariana of Spain ordered the construction of a sturdier fort to replace the wooden one. It was to be made from coquina stone. It was protected from being taken over by other enemies until 1819 when Spain gave control of Florida to the United States."

Piper and Emmerson, along with several other pupils, were beginning to get a little bored. It was very hot and humid, and the guide began to pick up on the students' restlessness. He stood on top of a nearby bench so the class could see and hear him better. In a thundering voice, he yelled, "do you want to hear about all the spirits who live at the fort?" This instantly got the attention of everyone. They immediately stopped fidgeting and stared at the man before them. He went on.

"Fifteen battles and sieges have been waged at this fortress. It's also still home to many who lived and died here over the past 300 hundred years. Night watchmen at the fort have reported seeing ghostly figures of Spanish soldiers patrolling the grounds.

Many members of the Apache and Seminole Indian Tribes died within the fortress, and they roam the halls, their spirits forever restless. Visitors have said to have seen lights glowing inside the watchtower at night. Also, a Spanish soldier appears to stand on the edge of the fortress, staring out to sea........ Now, let's go visit the dungeons!"

Everyone was now becoming excited about the tour guide's new interesting direction of the story telling. They followed him eagerly.

Once crammed into the small room, which was damp and musty smelling, Senga immediately began to feel unwell. She remembered it was the same feeling she had when she visited the Inveraray Jail in Scotland. Piper sensed her friend's discomfort and took hold of her arm.

"Senga, you look a bit weird, are you OK?" she asked gently.

"Not really," whispered Senga, trying not to draw attention to herself. "I just need to go outside, it's so hot in here."

The guide continued to entertain the boys and girls with more tales of prisoners and gruesome tortures while Senga began to back out of the dungeon in search of fresh air. All at once, she was enveloped in a strong, sickly, perfume. She felt like she could barely breathe, the scent was so powerful. She sensed something brush up against her and a mighty chill fell all over her body. She thought she was about to pass out. She quickly exited the dungeon and found her way into the courtyard again. The other students and the teacher weren't far behind her, followed by the tour guide, who was still talking. He was telling the class about Dolores, the young wife of a Spanish Colonel who lived at the fort with her husband. Supposedly she fell into his bad graces, and she was 'made to disappear.' When anyone asked the Colonel the whereabouts of his wife, he used the excuse that his wife had fallen ill and had gone back to Spain. Years later, however, her skeleton was found in a secret dungeon, and she continued to walk the grounds of the fort, leaving behind the sweet scent of the flowery perfume she always wore.

Senga knew at once that she'd just encountered Dolores. Once again, the spirit world had crossed paths with her!

Chapter Two

The St Augustine Lighthouse.

Senga, Piper, and Emmerson, along with their classmates, were back on the air-conditioned school bus and headed toward their next destination, the St Augustine Lighthouse. It was only a ten-minute ride, but Senga was happy to be on the move again. She was beginning to recover from her experience in the dungeon. She continued to sip on bottled water and looked out the window. She could now see the black and white lighthouse in the distance stretching up through the trees. Soon the students were piling out of the bus, chattering loudly. Another tour guide was waiting for them to show them around. First, they were to climb the tower. The guide assured them it was the best view in town! Two hundred and nineteen steps later, Senga, Piper and Emmerson, a little breathless, were at the top enjoying the lovely scenery. The tour guide, a petite little grandmotherly type was talking a mile a minute in a very animated manner. She filled everyone in on the history of the lighthouse, the shipwrecks, and the lives of the keepers and their families. One story caught the attention of all the students. It was about the Pittee girls. Mary 15, Eliza 13, and Carrie 4. Their father oversaw the lighthouse construction in 1871. In 1873 the three sisters and a friend were playing at the site. One of their favorite things to do was to ride a wooden cart down to the water's edge. One day, the cart carrying the four girls flipped into the water, trapping them below the surface. One of the workers saw the accident and raced to their side, but by the time he lifted the cart off the children, three of them had drowned. Only the youngest sister, Carrie, survived. Senga's classmates all groaned at hearing this sad story. Emmerson looked like she was about to cry.

"Well, I will cheer you all up now and take you to the gift shop," laughed their tour guide. Off they all trotted, looking forward to making some fun purchases.

Senga wandered around the cute shop checking out the books and knickknacks. She wanted to buy a little gift for her grandmother. Her eyes rested on a sweet little music box. It was wooden and had a painting of the lighthouse on the lid. Senga looked at the price tag. 'EEK!' It was way more than she could afford right now. She reluctantly put the box down and moved on to check out some china mugs. All of a sudden, the lid of the music box flipped open, and it started to play a tune. Senga turned to stare at it.

That was weird, she thought to herself. The lid had a little clasp attachment, and she knew that she'd closed and locked it properly.

Just then an assistant walked over. She closed the lid and fastened the catch. Senga smiled at her and moved on to look at the t-shirts. A few seconds later the music started again. Senga looked over at the box. Once again, the lid had flipped open! The assistant went over and picked up the music box. She looked at Senga with a strange expression.

"I promise you, I didn't touch that box again," exclaimed Senga.

The young girl stared at Senga.

"I know you didn't, it just happens sometimes."

"How do you mean?" asked a puzzled Senga.

The assistant smiled.

"Did you hear a story from the tour guide about the Pittee girls?"

"Oh yes, it was so sad," answered Senga.

"Well," said the girl, "We have many strange things that occur in and around the lighthouse, and we believe that the spirits of the young girls who drowned are trying to let everyone know that they're still present. For example, the music boxes play by themselves. This happens A LOT!"

Senga stared at the girl. "Really?" She responded softly. "What else?"

"There have been many sightings of the sisters by visitors. One day there was a group of British guests. At the end of their tour, someone from a different group complimented one of the British ladies on her little girl's perfect behavior, and how she was so patient to stay really close to her side during the guided tour. To which the British lady replied, puzzled, "but I don't have a little girl!"

Some nights when the staff is locking up, they hear giggling from different areas of the lighthouse. As though children are playing. Small, wet footsteps are sometimes found on the lighthouse steps and the floors in the morning when we open to the public. All very strange, but common occurrences around here."

Senga was taking in all this information. She was hardly surprised to hear what the girl was telling her, but at the same time, the hair on the back of her neck was standing on end.

Her teacher came into the gift shop to round up all the students. Senga, joined by Piper and Emmerson, made their way back to the bus. Senga hadn't been able to buy a gift after all, but she felt as though she'd just had another special experience and that felt like a gift in itself. As the bus slowly rolled out of the parking lot, she took one last look up at the beautiful lighthouse. There, at the very top leaning over the railing and waving with all their might, were three young girls!!

Chapter Three

Scotland bound!

Senga rolled over in her bed and glanced at the clock on the bedside table. Today was the day she was leaving for another trip to Scotland. She was beyond excited! This time Gran wasn't going. She and Papa were on an Alaskan cruise to celebrate a special anniversary. Her cousin Tony was accompanying her, and they were going to stay with Aunt Rena and Uncle Alex in Dunoon.

Part of the vacation was going to be spent in the Scottish Highlands. She and Tony were having a few days at a pony trekking center.

This was the first time Senga would be back in the Highlands since she had first met the MacBean family. She was a little nervous, but she couldn't contain her excitement at the same time. She had to find out what had happened when she found herself transported back to 1955! She knew it hadn't just been a dream. Finding the name, Weston Quin Barr MacBean at the Glasgow airport was just too much of a coincidence. She had to track this young man down so she could have some answers. She had found a W. MacBean online, but she wasn't sure if it was the same person. He was listed as living in Inverness, but she couldn't find an address. She was forming a plan that she fervently hoped would work out.

Now her cases were all packed and ready. Dad put everything into the car, and soon she and her parents were driving over to pick up Tony. She was ready for them and immediately jumped into the back seat to join her cousin. Waving goodbye to Tony's Mom and Dad, both girls started chatting eagerly with one another. Tony was dressed in her usual attire. Black leggings, black sweatshirt, and combat boots, with a dark green hoodie tied around her waist. Her beautiful hair was longer than Senga had ever seen it. However, she rarely wore it down and as usual, it was piled on top of her head in a wild but cute arrangement.

Senga was wearing light blue jeans, a baby pink t-shirt, and a white denim jacket. Her hair too had grown much longer. She had attempted to pull the thick mane back into a ponytail, but little curls were springing up all over her face, protesting the restriction.

After many hugs and kisses, and promises to be careful, the two girls were now at their departure gate. Tony purchased her usual candy bars and some magazines for the plane ride. Senga found a new paperback that she'd been dying to read and some gum.

Before too long their flight was being called and the girls made their way to the plane. They had a window and a middle seat.

"Senga, you take the middle seat please!!!" Pleaded Tony. "I hate sitting next to strangers."

"OK," laughed her cousin. She was used to giving Tony her way. She was a bit of a pain at times but fortunately, Senga was patient and good-natured and usually didn't mind keeping her happy. They settled into their seats.

Eventually the doors on the plane were closed and both girls realized, happily, that there would be a spare seat next to them.

Senga reached for her backpack which was stashed under the seat in front of her. Unzipping the side pouch, she removed her cherished Nessie

Stone, which by this time, was beginning to show a little wear. It wasn't nearly as shiny. The black paint faded to more of a dark grey shade. The Highland Cow and the sheep were barely recognizable, but Nessie was still proudly "swimming" along the water with her cheeky smile. Senga looked lovingly at her precious stone and popped it into her jacket's top pocket.

Tony had already departed to the 'Land of Nod.' Hoodie covering most of her face, earphones on, and the window shade closed. Senga looked down at her cousin. Some things never change, she thought, smiling. She too snuggled down into her seat, closed her eyes, and drifted off thinking of Scotland and all the great adventures that were sure to await them.

Chapter Four

Dunoon Glorious Dunoon.

Senga and Tony were enjoying the start of their summer holiday. Dunoon weather was being very kind to them. They were even going for swims in the River Clyde every day. Aunt Rena and Uncle Alex were delighted to have the girls stay with them and had been enjoying taking them for daily excursions in the car.

Today they were going to walk into town to do some shopping and enjoy a bite of lunch. They were both excited at the prospect of perhaps seeing Dasla and Tarla in their shop again. At the weekend they were driving up to Inverness to spend a few days at the pony trekking center. Senga could barely breathe every time she thought about it. Not only were they going to be riding every day, but Inverness was where the young artist, Weston, lived. She desperately wanted to track him down and get some answers. She had been thinking constantly about how she could accomplish this without Tony knowing about it.

They helped Aunt Rena clean up the kitchen after breakfast and then headed out for their walk. It was another beautiful day. The girls were already getting lovely suntans.

"What shall we do first, Tony?"

"I say, let's try to find the girls," responded Tony.

"I agree! I just can't wait to see them again!" Senga said excitedly. Off the two of them went, chattering and bantering all the way into town.

Chapter Five

The Shops.

The girls were almost at the beginning of town. Their pace picked up as they grew closer to the little clothing store where they had first met the girls. Senga opened the door, and they walked in. Just as it was last time, the shop was dimly lit. After being in the bright sunlight it took a while for their eyes to become accustomed. There were one or two other customers browsing. Suddenly both Senga and Tony spotted Dasla. She was attending to a young woman who was purchasing a top. Dasla looked up and saw the girls. She screamed with delight and ran over to them both, giving them huge hugs. She turned back to her bemused customer.

"I'm so sorry, Heather, I'll be right with you, I just haven't seen my friends in quite a while." She stepped back from Senga and Tony, still holding onto their hands.

"Hang on, I have to get Tarla, she will be so excited."

With that, she disappeared into the back of the shop. A few seconds later, both girls trotted back out. Again, more squealing and exuberant laughter all around.

"Sorry, let me get back to ringing up Heather, we'll chat in a minute." Dasla made her way back to the counter while the three girls continued to giggle and catch up. Just then, the door opened, and a beautiful sight was before them. Senga gasped in amazement; she couldn't believe her eyes. It was Erdra!!

Chapter Six

Meeting Erdra.

Senga realized she couldn't give the game away in front of Tony. Erdra had appeared to both in Selkie and human form on their last visit to Dunoon, but Tony had no recollection of that. However, she clearly was seeing the beautiful lady standing before her now. She just stared for the longest time. Dasla broke in to stop the awkward silence between them all.

"Girls, this is our mother, she is helping us in the shop just now. Mum this is Senga and Tony, the American girls we were telling you about. They're visiting again."

Erdra smiled at Senga and Tony.

"Hi girls! It's so nice to meet you both. My name is Erdra. My daughters told me so much about you when you were here on your last visit."

Senga glanced over at Tony, wondering if she'd remember the encounter at the west bay. She didn't seem to. She was staring at Erdra as though she couldn't quite take her in.

"Pleased to meet you, Erdra," Tony had finally found her voice.

"Hello, Erdra," smiled Senga. Giving the beautiful lady a knowing look and a silent *thank you* for handling the situation so well.

"Mum, would you mind if we took the girls to lunch?" asked Tarla. "We won't be gone long."

"Of course not, you girls go enjoy yourselves. Hopefully, I'll see you again before you return home, Senga and Tony." The cousins smiled and nodded their heads. "We'd love that," Senga said softly.

Erdra made her way over to the cash register area and proceeded to help the other customers who had begun to line up with their purchases. The four girls made their way to the doors and stepped out into the sunshine.

Chapter Seven

Lunch and a Catch-Up.

They walked to a little cafe at the end of the town overlooking the beautiful Clyde River. The girls ordered sandwiches, chips, cakes, and cans of Irn Bru, then started chattering all at once.

They caught up on what they'd all been doing since they had last seen one another. Dasla was in her last year of Grammar school and was planning on going to college in Glasgow to study art and design. She had a boyfriend and seemed very happy. Tarla didn't want to go to college. She planned to take over running the shop. She had no desire to move away from Dunoon. Erdra's name didn't come up in the conversations and Senga thought she should leave that topic well alone.

An hour had just flown, and soon, it was time for Dasla and Tarla to return to the shop. They promised one another that they'd get together before Senga and Tony returned to the States.

"Have a great time at your pony trekking place," smiled Tarla. "I'm so envious, I wish I could go with you."

"Yes, enjoy!" echoed Dasla. "Just take lots of midge spray. Those wee devils are murder, and you'll get eaten alive."

Both girls laughed and thanked her for the advice, then, they went their separate ways.

Senga and Tony wandered back along the promenade, enjoying the gorgeous views.

"Wonder what Aunt Rena is making for tea?" Tony looked at Senga who had just burst out laughing. "What's so funny?"

"Oh, Tony, you just had a ginormous sandwich, chips, a cream cake, and a huge drink and now you're thinking about your tea?"

Both girls started laughing, and arm in arm, they proceeded on their journey.

Chapter Eight

Inverness.

Senga and Tony woke up bright and early on the day they were to drive to Inverness. Aunt Rena and Uncle Alex were dropping them off at the pony trekking center and then going on a little sightseeing trip of their own. It was a four-hour journey so both girls came prepared with snacks, pillows, blankets, and movies downloaded onto their tablets. It was a lovely drive, and the sun shone the whole way. After stopping for lunch and several other detours along the way they arrived at the center. It was more like a farm, and it reminded Senga of the MacBean's home. Uncle Alex pulled up to the front door of the main house. A cheery-looking teenage girl popped out the front door to greet them.

"Hello, I'm Mirren, welcome to Stoneybrook!"

Everyone piled out of the car and shook Mirren's hand. Uncle Alex pulled the girls' cases from the trunk, and they all followed Mirren into the house and down a long, hallway.

"This is your room, girls," said Mirren opening the door wide to let the group troop inside. It was a lovely space with two full-size beds adorned with plush pillows and comfy-looking duvets. It had a large window letting in lots of natural light and capturing the beauty of the many paintings of Highland ponies hanging on the walls.

Tony threw herself down on one of the beds and kicked off her boots. "Wow, this bed is amazing! So soft and squishy." Senga laughed,

"well, I guess I'm having this one then," as she sat on the edge of the other bed to test the comfort level.

"Right then, girls, we'll be off," smiled Aunt Rena, after making sure her nieces had everything they needed. She bent down to give each of them a kiss on the cheek. "We'll be back to pick you up in four days. Have a great time and please be careful!" The girls promised they would and affectionately hugged their aunt and uncle goodbye.

Senga soon had all her clothes and toiletries unpacked and neatly stashed in the drawers provided. Tony, on the other hand, her side of the room looked like a bomb had gone off. Clothes and stuff everywhere.

"Oh geez, come on girlfriend, get your act together," moaned Senga, rolling her eyes. She started to help get her cousin organized and soon the room was all spic and span again. They both changed into jeans, sweatshirts, and boots and left the room to go exploring.

Chapter Nine

The Ponies.

The girls wandered outside and walked toward what looked like a line of stalls. Upon closer inspection, they were both delighted to find the stables were being occupied by the most darling ponies. One by one, nosy little heads popped over the barn doors. Senga and Tony stopped by each one, nuzzling their velvety noses and oohing and aahing over them all. Just then, several young women appeared in the courtyard.

"Hello," called out one. "Are you ready for a hack?" She smiled at the girls.

Tony nudged Senga in the ribs, "Hack? What the heck is a hack?"

Senga laughed, "oh she's just asking if we want to go for a ride."

"Why the heck did she not just say that then?" chuckled her cousin cheekily.

Just then, several other guests started appearing in the courtyard. One of the stable hands walked up to the girls.

"Is this your first day?" she asked cheerily.

"Yes," nodded Senga, "we just arrived a short time ago. Can you tell us which ponies are still available for us to ride?"

"Of course, and my name is Anne. The other girls," she pointed in the direction of the additional stable hands, "that's Fiona with the dark hair, Morven is the blonde one. We are here to help in any way we can and to take you on some great hacks. Have you both ridden before?"

"Me, not so much," Tony answered sheepishly, "but Senga, she's an awesome rider." Senga blushed at the compliment, "well, I'm not sure about *awesome* but I've had a bit more experience than Tony here."

Anne beckoned Senga and Tony over to the two stalls at the end of the stables. "Well, no worries, girls." We have ponies here for all levels. Better start you out with old Maggie, Tony. She's very gentle and she hates going any faster than a slow trot." She opened the door to the stall and all three girls walked in to meet Maggie. She was a plump little cream mare with a long forelock hiding her eyes. She immediately started to rub her nose up and down Tony's arm, hoping for a snack.

"Aw, she likes you, Tony," said Senga encouragingly. She knew her cousin was a little bit nervous.

Tony was clearly relieved at how friendly the pony was behaving toward her. She reached her hand up to rub Maggie's ears. "Oh, she's so cute," she murmured. "I love her already."

"Great, that's you sorted then," laughed Anne. "I'll help you get the tack on and go over a few things with you. Senga, if you pop next door, you'll meet Fergus. He's got a wee bit more life about him, so he'll keep you on your toes. From what you've told me, I think you'll be a good match for him."

Senga was excited to meet her pony. She unlatched the door and was met by a beauty. A chestnut with a silver mane and tail. Anne had followed her into the stall.

"Isn't he stunning?"

"Oh my gosh, yes!" I have never seen a Highland with these colors before."

"No, they are only bred on the island of Rum," said Heather, stroking the pony's head. We are very lucky to have Fergus. He's been a great addition to our stables. Can I leave you to tack up, Senga? I'll pop next door and check on Tony."

"Oh sure," smiled Senga. "We'll be just fine," as she reached for the saddle and began to prepare for their first ride together. She was so excited!!

Chapter Ten

The Rainy Day.

The girls had been on long hacks for the last two days and had thoroughly enjoyed themselves. Tony had been a quick learner and was already looking quite the experienced rider. Senga was very proud of her. On the third day, they woke up to torrential rain pounding off their bedroom windows.

Tony stretched lazily under her covers while Senga jumped up to the window to survey the severity of the weather.

"Well, it's not looking too promising out there," Senga announced cheerily. She was actually happy that it was raining, she had been forming a plan in her head to try to go into town without Tony. She had to find Weston MacBean. This was her last opportunity as they were leaving in the morning to go back to Dunoon.

"No riding today, I would imagine," said Senga, in what she hoped was a disappointed-sounding voice.

"That's OK," responded Tony, snuggling back under her quilt. "I've discovered muscles I never knew I had. I'm quite stiff and sore all over. I think a nice hot soak in the bathtub is in my immediate future."

Senga laughed at her cousin. "Well, you know you use eight key muscles when you ride a horse. No wonder you feel sore."

Just at that, there was a soft knock on the door. Senga opened it to find Anne standing there with a collection of pamphlets and maps. She handed them to Senga and stepped into the room.

"Morning, girls, I'm so sorry about the weather. The forecast isn't looking good, I'm afraid. It's supposed to be like this until tomorrow. We'll have to call off the riding, for today at least. However, there is still plenty to do, and I've brought you some brochures to check out. There is a minibus leaving in an hour to take you into town if you'd like to get out."

Senga's eyes lit up. *Just what she wanted to hear*, she thought. *Now if only she could go into town alone....*

"What would you like to do, Tony? she turned to her cousin, who was still in her bed.

"I think I'm going to go back to sleep for a while," announced Tony sleepily. Then after my bath I'll just relax today. Probably watch a few movies. What do you feel like doing?"

"Actually, I'd love to go into town and do a little shopping, if you don't mind?" She needn't have worried, Tony had already turned on her side and drifted off, snoring softly into her pillow. Senga and Anne looked at one another and chuckled softly.

Chapter Eleven

The Hunt.

Senga was excitedly scanning all the shops as the minibus pulled up to the High Street shopping area. She was the first person out of the bus, and she quickly made her way down the left-hand side of the street. Her eyes were scanning the store names, hoping with all her might that she would see something with a MacBean reference. There were boutiques, cafes, bookstores, etc., but it was the Scottish shops displaying unique local artistry with which she was mainly focused. She popped into the first one that looked promising. The window display was full of small paintings with Scottish scenery. She walked up to the lady behind the cash register. She reminded Senga of her beloved gran, and she instantly had a pang of missing her.

"Good morning, my dear, how are you?" smiled the Gran lookalike.

"Very well, thank you," responded Senga politely. "I'm wondering if you can help me. I'm looking for a young artist. His name is Weston MacBean. Have you heard of him by any chance?" The lady shook her head at Senga, "I'm sorry Pet, that name doesn't ring a bell with me. However, there are quite a few shops in the town, maybe you'll have better luck there." Senga, nodding and thanking her, made her way back into the street. She popped into half a dozen more shops, asking the same question and getting the same response. She was beginning to get tired and feeling a little hopeless. It's pointless she thought, I'll never find this boy. It's like looking for a needle in a haystack. She was almost at the end of the town now, having walked down both sides of the street. She glanced at the name on the last shop window. It was called 'Inverness Artisans.' She went inside. It was a huge store with what appeared to be individual stalls with various sorts of crafts and artwork displayed. She wandered her way down the first aisle. There was jewelry, quilts, baby clothes, pet items, furniture, knitted goods, on and on it went. She was almost at the back of the store now. A few people were milling around. She stopped to speak to a young woman who was hanging some beaded necklaces onto a display board.

"Excuse me, please," Senga said softly, not wishing to startle the girl. The young woman turned around and smiled at Senga. "Yes?" Suddenly Senga's mouth dropped open and her eyes were wide as saucers. She was staring over the girl's right shoulder. There, in the next stall was a large white wooden sign hanging on the wall. It said in large, navy blue, curvy, font, 'WQBM Scottish Arts and Crafts.' Her eyes darted over to the corner of the stall. There, hanging all over a wooden picket fence was a myriad of small, painted pieces of slate with Scottish landscapes. On an adjacent display case lay numerous painted stones. Senga moved closer to the stall and picked up a stone. It was smooth, shiny, and black. About three inches long, two inches wide, and half an inch thick. On the right top-hand corner was a Highland Cow, on the left top corner was a wooly sheep, and taking up most of the space in the middle was a light grey 'Nessie,' swimming cheekily along the water, AND she was smiling!!!!!!!

Chapter Twelve

Weston.

Senga's knees began to buckle underneath her. She'd found him!!! Well, almost! At least she'd found the place where he worked. She turned to the girl in the next stall again. "I'm sorry to bother you once more, do you happen to know the owner of this booth?"

"Oh yes, of course, West!" She smiled, "he should be back in a few. He just popped out for a quick bite of lunch. However, if you want to purchase any of his work, just take it to the front reception area and they'll ring it up for you." Senga felt faint. *He should be back in a few!*

Shortly her life was about to change, and she wasn't 100% sure she was ready to ask the questions that needed to be asked or hear the answers.

"Thanks a lot, said Senga cheerfully, hoping that her wobbly voice wouldn't give anything away. She proceeded to walk around the rest of the exhibits, not seeing a thing, everything was swimming in front of her eyes and her mind was racing. She turned the corner at the front of the store and ran smack-bang into a tall young man. He had on faded blue jeans, and a grey V-neck tee shirt. She would have recognized him anywhere. Not only did he look exactly like the photograph she saw at the airport, but he was also Bobby's double!

"Oh, I'm really sorry!" Senga blurted out, for want of something better to say.

"Och, you're fine, lass, he chuckled down at her. "Where's the fire though?"

"The...the fire?" stammered Senga.

He laughed." Aye, you're going at breakneck speed, I thought maybe the back of the shop had burst into flames." His Scottish accent was quite strong, but she could also detect another dialect in there. She couldn't quite put her finger on it.

She laughed nervously.

"I was just admiring your work. Here's a funny story. My gran has an identical stone. The black-painted one with Nessie, the highland cow, pony, Scottish flag, and sheep. As a matter of fact, she gave it to me for good luck while I'm here on holiday." She pulled it from her pocket and held it out in the palm of her hand. "Hi, by the way, I'm Senga."

The young man stared at the stone, his eyes widening. Even as faded as it was, he appeared to recognize the similarities right away.

"Wow!" He exclaimed. "That certainly looks like one of my stones. Hi Senga, I'm Weston. Everyone calls me West. Nice to meet you. Is that an American accent I hear?"

Senga felt as though she was having an out-of-body experience. She was trying hard to hold it together and not let Weston see that she was completely rattled.

"Yes, I'm American, from Florida actually. My Gran is from Dunoon and I'm visiting my aunt and uncle who live there. I'm here in Inverness until tomorrow. My cousin, Tony and I have been staying at Stoneybrook for the last three days." She blurted it all out before she realized it.

"Oh, Stoneybrook! That's a lovely place. I know the owners. My family used to live here a few generations ago, but they all emigrated to

Australia in the early 60's. I decided to move back a couple of years ago.

Once again, Senga's heart started to race at the mention of Weston's family.

Years ago, my grandad used to paint the stones and sell them in his aunt's shop in the wee town where he lived, not too far from here. I wonder if that's where your gran found her stone? He was a wonderful artist. I think that's where I developed my love of drawing and painting."

Senga took a big gulp and with a quivering voice whispered, "is he still alive?"

"Oh aye, very much so. In fact, my grandad and my dad are here from Australia visiting me just now."

Senga wasn't sure how much more information she could take. It was like watching a movie run at top speed inside her head.... *Bobby was here in Inverness!!*

Chapter Thirteen

Older Bobby.

Senga had managed to pull herself together. She felt very guilty about telling Weston a little white lie, but to find out more about Bobby she had to try to get closer to the young man. She had quickly devised a story to say that her gran may have known Bobby and his family as she used to holiday in the area every year. Weston had suggested that Senga join them for an early dinner, to which she had eagerly agreed. They were to meet at a restaurant in town in an hour. Senga had time to call Tony at Stoneybrook and tell her she'd be arriving back a little later than she thought as she was still shopping. Another white lie!!! She was feeling very guilty about having to be dishonest, it wasn't her nature, but she also knew that she had no choice if she wanted to get more answers. Tony was just fine and perfectly content. She had been enjoying having a lazy day and resting her sore joints. She relayed to Senga that a minibus would be picking her up at 7:30.

Senga spent the next forty-five minutes wandering through the town again. She quickly picked up a few odds and ends so Tony wouldn't wonder why she was returning empty handed. After pacing up and down the town it was time to head for the restaurant. She opened the front door and was met by a cheery hostess. Senga told her she was meeting friends and the young lady showed her to a table over by a large window. The restaurant was already beginning to fill up. She was anxiously staring at the entrance each time the door opened. Just a few minutes after five in walked Weston. Behind him, two gentlemen. The first was tall, neatly attired in a dark suit and a mass of silver hair. A much older version of Weston. Senga had literally stopped breathing. She was now looking at whom she presumed to be Bobby. Behind him, Weston's dad, shorter, with reddish hair and rosy cheeks. Senga thought he looked just like Mrs MacBean.

Weston scanned the room, then saw Senga and ushered the two older men over to her table. Her knees were knocking, and she was relieved that she was sitting down. She looked up at the three men and smiled. Weston made quick introductions and they took their seats. Senga was trying hard not to stare at Bobby. There didn't seem to be any signs of recognition when their eyes met. She saw right away that he still had the most startling blue eyes. Although his once jet-black hair was now silver, it was styled neatly. His lined face was deeply tanned. *He is still so handsome,* thought Senga who was trying hard not to become emotional.

Weston's Dad, Quin, began to ask all sorts of questions about Florida and Senga's connections to Scotland. She filled them all in as best she could.

Then it was her turn. She found out that Bobby's Mum and Dad, had sold their farm in 1960, just five years after she'd met them, and the family had moved out to Australia. Mr MacBean's cousin lived there, and he helped them to get settled, before eventually purchasing another farm which had been very successful. Bobby had gone to university to become an engineer. Weston was clearly very proud of his grandfather's accomplishments. He told Senga that he had been part of a small team of engineers who had designed some sort of very important, medical, equipment. It was a kind of x-ray machine that resulted in many lives being saved due to the invention. Jean and Mary were both still alive and doing very well with large families of their own. Senga was extremely happy to hear that and soaking up all the wonderful news. She wasn't a bit surprised to hear how successful the family had become in their new lives in Australia. However, she was very sad to come to the realization that Bobby's mind seemed to be a little fuzzy. He kept getting mixed up with names and places. He was struggling to remember the past and becoming quite confused. It broke Senga's heart to watch him wrestle with his words. Weston, however, was incredibly patient and kind with his grandad, quietly soothing and appeasing him. Once again, Senga could feel a lump come to her throat. How emotional to see Bobby like this, but how wonderful that he had such a caring, loving grandson like Weston.

All too soon it was time for Senga to go. The three men walked her to the corner of town where she was to meet the bus. Weston put his hand inside his leather jacket and pulled out a small package wrapped in tissue paper. He handed it to Senga.

"What's this?" she asked, in a surprised voice.

"Just a wee memento to take back home with you, also, I've given you my contact information on a card. I hope we can stay in touch."

"Oh wow, thank you very much," she responded softly. "Yes, I would love to stay in touch."

Just then the minibus rolled up to the curb. She gave Weston and his dad a hug, then turned to Bobby. She looked into his beautiful eyes, and he stared back at her intently. She thought for sure that she saw a glimmer of recognition pass over his face, but then it was gone. He kissed Senga gently on the cheek.

"Cheerio, Lass. It was lovely to meet you!"

Senga's emotions came rushing to the surface and she knew she needed to leave them. She jumped onto the bus and quickly settled in one of the front seats. She looked out at the three men through her tears, which were by now cascading down her cheeks. She smiled bravely at them and waved until the bus turned the corner and they were out of sight. She looked at the small package in her lap and slowly began to open the tissue paper. Inside was a bright, new, shiny, Nessie stone, a business card and a recent photograph of Weston, his dad and his grandfather. All three had their arms around one another and were smiling widely into the camera. Senga was so elated to have it. She pulled the original stone out of her jacket pocket and compared the two. It was almost identical to the one Bobby had given her in 1955. The only difference was, Weston had added his initials on the reverse side.   She placed them both inside her pocket, closed her eyes and thought about what she was going to tell Tony when she returned to Stoneybrook.

Chapter Fourteen

The Plan.

Aunt Rena and Uncle Alex picked the girls up the next day, and soon they were safely back in Dunoon. Tony had been keeping the conversation going for most of the journey, and for that, Senga was very grateful. She had woken up feeling so sad and forlorn. It had been wonderful to see Bobby again, even all these years later, but it made her miss the MacBean family even more. She and Weston had promised to stay in touch though, so she was extremely happy that she could at least keep up to date with how everyone was doing.

After unpacking and eating a light lunch the girls decided to walk into town again. They were eager to meet up with Dasla and Tarla once more before they returned to the States. Upon reaching the little boutique Tony announced that she wanted to check out another little shop further down the street. She told Senga to go ahead and that she would meet her shortly. The shop was empty of customers, but Senga spotted Erdra immediately who greeted her warmly.

"Hello, beautiful girl! It's lovely to see you again. I'm sorry my two aren't here right now though."

Senga was disappointed, but she decided she would take the opportunity to speak to Erdra about the MacBean family. She just needed to speak to someone who would understand, not freak out about all the weird things Senga had encountered. She also had to talk quickly, as she didn't want Tony to walk in and hear any of their conversation. Erdra listened intently as Senga gave her a brief rundown of everything that had happened since she had first encountered the family in the Highlands back in 1955, as well as running into Weston and Bobby in Inverness. Once she came up for air, Erdra responded kindly.

"Sweet girl, I have always known that you had special powers, I told you so that first day we met. It's a wonderful gift to have, but yet, it does come with many obstacles, and trying moments that will be hard for you to overcome sometimes. What can I do to help?"

Senga was very touched by the Selkie's concern for her. It was such a relief to finally share her experiences with someone who could understand and not judge her.

"I was hoping you could help me return to see the MacBean family again. Back to 1955."

Erdra gave Senga a long, serious stare. Her large, beautiful eyes were looking right into the girl's soul.

"Do you really want to do such a thing, my love? It's a bit dangerous. You were very lucky last time that you were able to come back. Many people get stuck in the past, or the future, and they can't return to their present-day lives again. Are you willing to take that risk?"

Senga thought for a second, then nodded her head slowly. "I am willing, Erdra. I feel such a pull to go back there, I'm not sure why but I just know I must try."

"OK, Lovely. I will help you." Erdra hugged her young friend and whispered softly in her ear, "be at the spot where you and I first met, at 7 pm tonight. I'll take you to where you need to be."

Senga hugged the Selkie tightly and whispered back, "thank you Erdra, this means more to me than you can imagine." Just then,

Tony appeared, loaded down with shopping bags and looking rather pleased with herself.

"Looks like you had a successful shopping spree, Coz. OK, let's head home now, Aunt Rena will be getting our tea ready." Cheery goodbyes were exchanged with Erdra, and the two girls made their way out of the shop. Tony was excitedly giving Senga a rundown of all the gifts she'd purchased for family and friends at home. Her cousin was barely listening. All she could think about was meeting Erdra in a few hours and the chance in a lifetime experience that lay ahead of her. She was both terrified and elated all at the same time!!

Chapter Fifteen

The Unicorn.

It was five minutes to seven as Senga walked quickly along the prom towards the area where she and Erdra first met. She was wearing a small backpack containing a change of clothes, toiletries, her wallet, the photo of the MacBean men and the two stones. She had told her aunt and uncle that her friend, Dasla, had invited her to spend the night. She had no idea how things were going to pan out. She wanted to make sure she had enough time to avoid worrying her family. Tony had been a bit annoyed that she hadn't been invited too.

"Why didn't Tarla want me to come," she asked rather huffily.

"Well, apparently she had already made plans ages ago to visit a friend in Glasgow. I'm sorry, Coz."

"Don't you worry, Pet," said her aunt comfortingly, putting her arm around her niece. "You and I will make a big bowl of popcorn and watch some girly films all night. What do you think?"

Tony gave a weak smile, trying to pretend that she wasn't in the least bit interested in doing that. However, she hugged her aunt back and chimed in with, "and we can make hot fudge sundaes too?!" Aunt Rena chuckled and ruffled Tony's already messy hair. "You got it, Kid!"

Senga was out of breath by the time she reached the spot where she had agreed to meet Erdra. She could see the lovely lady already there on the beach waiting. She was sitting on a rock staring out at the beautiful Clyde. She jumped up when she heard the stones crunching behind her and quickly hugged Senga.

"Good girl, you're on time, now we need to get going."

She ushered Senga back up the shore and onto the promenade and the two started walking in the direction of the swing park. Upon reaching that, Erdra took her young friend's hand, and they crossed the road making their way to a wooded area. Until this point Senga had not asked any questions and Erdra had not offered any explanation as to where they were going. All Senga knew was that she trusted the Selkie completely. The woods were becoming a lot denser, and they were climbing higher above the town. Suddenly Erdra stopped walking, pulling Senga closer to her. She was looking all around them, eyes narrowing, looking off into the distance. Senga heard, before she saw anything. It was the distinct badum, badum, badum of horses' hooves. She knew and loved that sound; however, she wasn't quite prepared for the amazing vision that was now appearing very quickly before them. It had started to slow down as it got closer and then came to a complete stop on a little rise just above the two ladies. It was the most beautiful horse Senga had ever seen. It was a startling white. Had a majestic head with large blue eyes and a flowing, pearly-white, mane and tail. Although, it **wasn't** a horse!! This magnificent animal had a single, pointed, horn on its forehead. Senga had of course heard of Unicorns, but she never dreamed of ever actually seeing one in real life. Erdra was now speaking to the creature in a strange language Senga could not recognize. It almost sounded like gibberish but every now and then Senga could understand what she was saying. She heard her name mentioned several times also the MacBean family and 1955. The Unicorn was listening intently, occasionally tossing it's perfectly formed head and pawing the ground gently. Now Erdra turned her attention to Senga.

"All right, my brave girl, this is Vespera, he is going to take you back to visit with your special family, but you mustn't stay longer than twelve hours. That is all you are allowed, or it may be too difficult to bring you back. Do you understand?"

"I….I…I think so," stammered Senga. "How will I know where to meet him?"

"He will let you know all of that once you arrive at your destination. First things first. You trust me, right?"

"Of course, I do," replied Senga, vigorously nodding her head.

"All right then, let's get you on board." Erdra motioned for Senga to move over to Vespera's side and linked her long slender fingers together, palms up. Senga placed her left foot gently on top of Erdra's hands, grabbed a handful of silky mane and expertly pulled herself up on top of the Unicorn's back. It really wasn't any different than riding a pony bareback, she thought.

"How does that feel," asked Erdra, smiling up at her young friend.

"Senga tightened her fingers around Vespera's mane and smiled down at Erdra. "It's very comfortable really," responded Senga, returning the smile bravely.

"Take good care of my sweet friend, Vespera," said Erdra softly, gently stroking the side of his neck. The Unicorn nodded his head a couple of times then slowly turned around and began to walk into the woods.

Chapter Sixteen

Where It All Began.

Senga could feel the Unicorn begin to pick up the pace. He was now at a flat-out gallop. Trees and shrubbery were flying by them at an alarming rate. She lowered her head and was almost laying across the animal's strong neck. She felt strangely comfortable and secure though. Almost lulled into a hypnotic trance. She closed her eyes. She had no idea how much time had gone by, but she felt Vespera begin to slow down. He was now cantering along a green field. Senga raised her head and looked over the Unicorn's head. She could see some buildings in the distance, but otherwise the area looked very remote. The pace had now slowed down to a clipped trot then the Unicorn was walking. He came up alongside a stone wall and stopped. Senga sensed that she was to jump off, which she did. She felt rather stiff and a bit cold but otherwise none the worse for the wear. Vespera began to nudge her arm. She looked up at him and they locked eyes. She knew he was sending her a message. To be back in this same spot twelve hours from now. She nodded her acknowledgement and hugged his neck gratefully. Vespera tossed his head up in the air and gracefully took off, galloping once more across the field. Senga watched him until he disappeared then turned to look at the scenery before her. She thought it looked familiar, but she couldn't be sure. She began to walk in the direction of the buildings. She was glad she was dressed for the occasion. She had on short, comfortable, leather boots, black jeans and a thick dark blue sweatshirt. She reached up to smooth her hair. It was pulled back with an elastic but as usual her curls were popping out all over her cute face. She looked to the left, there was the stream, bubbling and lapping just like the first time she had seen it. She knew that the farmhouse was going to be there once she climbed over the stone wall in front of her. Yes, there it was! She could see smoke spiraling out of the chimney. She remembered the MacBeans had a cheery fire on the last time she saw them. She suddenly felt very weary, but she was incredibly excited to be back. She just hoped that it was in fact 1955 and that she could explain away why she'd just disappeared so suddenly. She was looking around for any signs of life. She could see the sheep on the hills above her but nothing else. She walked closer to the house and her tummy began to churn. She also realized that it had been absolute ages since she'd last eaten anything. She was ravenous! Just then the front door opened. Senga ducked behind an outhouse. She remembered it was where she had first met the darling puppies. She peeked around the side of the building and could see someone walk across the yard. It was Mrs MacBean! She had a wicker laundry basket on her left hip, and she was walking over to the clothesline where several sheets and pillowcases were wafting in the slight breeze. Senga stayed put. She didn't want to scare the dear lady and she was still at a loss as to what to say to explain her last abrupt departure. She waited patiently until the sheets and pillowcases were removed from the line and Mrs MacBean was back inside the house. Now what? Senga thought, helplessly. She could hardly go and knock on their door. 'Hi, there, I'm back again from the future and just wanted to stop by for a quick visit.' Nope, she needed a better plan. Just at that moment, she heard a vehicle driving up the dirt road in front of the house. It rolled into the yard and stopped close to where she was hiding. She folded herself back behind the building and waited patiently to hear a car door open, which it did. She peeked around the side of the building again and saw to her delight, the two girls exiting from the back seat of an old green van!!

Chapter Seventeen

Jean.

Senga wanted to scream their names at the top of her lungs, but she contained herself. Dearest Jean and Mary! She was over the moon to see them again. They were pulling bags from the back of the truck. Senga figured they must have been in town getting some groceries. Now she had a better look at the girls as they proceeded to walk across the courtyard toward the front door. *Wait a minute! The girls looked different. They were taller, both had really short hair curling around their ears. They just looked.....older!!!* The driver's door opened and out popped Mr MacBean. He still looked pretty much the same as the last time Senga had seen him. Maybe a little grayer. Senga was now realizing that this was probably not 1955. She leaned back against the cool stone of the building she was hiding behind and closed her eyes. *How in the world was she going to explain herself to them*? Her mind was racing. She just had to get the girls alone and tell them the truth. She would have to wait around and hope that one or both would exit the house sooner rather than later. She didn't have to wait long. The front door opened, and Jean came out carrying a bucket. She proceeded to walk across the courtyard and into an adjacent barn. Senga guessed that she was about to go feed an animal and that she was filling the bucket with grain of some sort. She was right, Jean exited almost right away, and Senga could tell from the way that she was walking that the bucket was now full. She followed Jean around the back of the barn and keeping her distance tried to figure out which direction she was going. She was headed down to a field and Senga knew instantaneously why. Suddenly three ponies appeared from a cluster of trees at the far end of the field and began cantering towards Jean. It was Coal, Dumpling and Caramel. Senga wanted to cry at the sight before her. She couldn't take the suspense any longer. She walked down to the gate near where Jean was standing with the ponies. Jean didn't turn around, but Coal suddenly alerted to someone getting close and that made Jean look over her shoulder. Senga slowly opened the gate and walked in, closing it behind her. The girls' eyes locked together, and both stood still like statues. All of a sudden, Jean dropped the bucket and ran over to Senga, screeching at the top of her lungs. They hugged for what seemed like ten minutes then pulled apart and stared at one another,

"Oh Senga, I can't believe you're here! We thought we'd never see you again. What happened? Where did you go? How did you get back here?"

Senga smiled at her friend and took a deep breath.

"Jean, you have no idea how much I've thought about you all since I left. To be honest I have not much information to give you. It's all still a mystery to me. I just remember falling off Dumpling and then I was back in Florida again. I've had to keep lots of things from my family and friends as they would think I'm quite simply bonkers!"

"Well, said Jean, "all I can tell you is that I had no clue what had happened to you. We were slightly in front, if you can remember. When I finally realized you weren't behind us, Dumpling had already headed back to the gate. By the time I reached her there was absolutely no sign of you at all. I searched for ages, calling your name. It was then that I realized you had probably disappeared as suddenly as you had appeared when we first met you. Bobby had ridden on, so he wasn't aware that you'd fallen off and I didn't tell him. When you didn't show up for dinner that night, I just explained to everyone that I'd walked you down to the bus stop as you were worried your folks might be missing you and needed to return to them. Everyone understood although they were sad you hadn't said cheerio. I did share with Mary what had happened, so she knows as much as I do. I did hate to tell fibs to everyone but what else could I do, Senga?"

"Oh, trust me, I definitely understand, Jean. I have had to tell so many white lies to my family and friends. However, nobody would understand or believe all the crazy things that have happened to me lately. I had lots of help returning to you today, but I only have twelve hours so not much time to catch up. I'll try to fill you in the best I can. By the way, what year is it?"

"July 23, 1958. Three years have passed since we last saw you! You've grown so much."

"You girls have too, responded Senga. I saw you both get out of your dad's car earlier. How is Bobby? Where is he?"

"Bobby is great. He's working down at our aunt's shop in town for the summer. He's still painting and selling his stones to all the tourists who come in. He will be so happy to see you again, Mary too! Come on, let's go to the house."

Jean finished feeding the ponies then putting her arm around Senga's shoulders the two girls started to walk back towards the farm.

Chapter Eighteen

The Reunion.

Senga followed Jean nervously into the farmhouse. They had decided to tell everyone that Senga was just back for one day to visit. She was immediately met by Mrs MacBean in the kitchen who gave a great whoop of excitement and embraced Senga in a giant hug.

"Oh my gracious, Lass! You're back!? We missed seeing you before you left last time. How long are you here?"

"Not very long, I'm afraid, Mrs MacBean. I have to leave again tomorrow. Headed back to Dunoon with my folks."

"Well, I'm so glad you could pop in and see us, Pet. You have to stay and have tea with us, I've made Shepherd's Pie."

"What's all the commotion? …. Oh, my goodness, Senga!!!! When did you get here?" Mary yelled at the top of her lungs as she entered the kitchen. She flew over to Senga and hugged and kissed her, almost knocking her off her feet.

"Hi Mary! It's so great to see you! I just arrived a short time ago. How are you?" Senga was elated to be back in this house with these wonderful people. She just hated that her time was going to be so short.

"Come on, let's go catch up," said Jean, grabbing Senga's hand and leading her out of the kitchen. Mary followed and the three girls galloped up the stairs. They now had separate rooms. Jean pulled Senga into hers and all three girls collapsed onto the bed and began chattering all at once. Of course, Jean and Mary had tons of questions about how Senga had just mysteriously disappeared so suddenly three years ago and what she'd been doing since that had happened. Senga patiently told them everything while her friends stared at her in amazement. She felt quite exhausted after a while and fell back onto the pillow, laughing up at Jean and Mary.

"OK, I've filled you in, now it's your turn, girls, tell me everything!"

"Crikey, Senga. Compared to your last few years, ours will sound pretty boring," laughed Jean.

"Oh, but we do have a bit of news," Mary joined in, her smile fading from her face.

"Tell me." said Senga, a little alarmed at the seriousness of Mary's tone.

"Mum and Dad want to move to Australia. Dad's brother has a farm out there and he's asked Dad to join him and help run it. None of us kids want to leave. Bobby especially is so upset. He's threatening not to go. He's eighteen now so he doesn't have to. Mum and Dad have been arguing a lot about it. It's been very stressful."

Senga stared at the girls for a few seconds then turned to her backpack. She pulled out her new stone and the photo that Weston had given her. Before showing them, she spoke in a solemn, low voice, she definitely didn't want anyone else to hear what she had to say.

"OK, girls, don't freak out but what I'm going to tell you is pretty incredible. You have to trust me though. Are you ready?"

Jean and Mary's faces had both turned a little pale. They were more than a little apprehensive about what they were about to hear.

Senga proceeded to tell the girls about being in Inverness recently. About how she'd tracked down a young man who had also painted Scottish scenes on rocks. She skirted around naming him until the very end of her story.

"The young man's name is Weston Quin Barr MacBean. He introduced me to his father, Quin and his grandfather, Bobby. She held up the photograph to the girls. Jean took it from her with quivering fingers, showing it to her sister. Both girls immediately started to cry softly. They turned to Senga and Mary whispered, "how is this possible?"

"I know, it's a huge shock, girls, I'm so sorry to do this to you. I just wanted to share it though because I know for a fact that you do ALL go to Australia, and you all love it there. Weston has come back to Inverness, but the rest of your family are still there living happily. I don't want you to worry because it will all work out. Somehow, we have to convince Bobby of this, so your family won't be so upset."

"Well, no time like the present," Jean announced quietly. "I can hear Bobby's voice downstairs. Come on ladies. We should help Mum get the tea ready."

Chapter Nineteen

Younger Bobby.

The girls trooped down the stairs and into the kitchen. Senga could hear Bobby's voice raised. He was arguing with his dad. He sounded angry and Senga was so surprised as she'd not expected he'd ever get upset in such a way. As the girls walked in on them both men turned in their direction. Bobby stopped talking immediately. He caught sight of Senga and his mood changed immediately.

"For goodness sake, would you look at this!" Bobby was now grinning from ear to ear. He walked over to Senga and ruffled her hair. He was towering above her now. He was even more handsome than Senga remembered. His startling eyes were more enhanced due to his dark tanned skin. His jet-black hair was a little longer, and still parted on one side.

"Hi Bobby." Senga smiled shyly. She felt like a little kid looking up at him. "I'm just back for a quick visit."

"Well, it's great to see you, Lass. I'll forgive you for not saying 'cheerio' the last time you were here. Jean told me you had to leave quite suddenly."

Senga blushed. "Ah, yes, I'm so sorry about that. I felt awful not being able to see you before I headed back."

Mr MacBean had been silent for this whole conversation. Just quietly observing in the corner of the kitchen. He now leaned forward and said in a loud voice. "Great, Senga's back, now, when do we eat, Mother?" Everyone laughed and Mrs MacBean tutted. "Oh Quin, where are your manners?" She rolled her eyes at her husband and good naturedly gave him a nudge on the arm. Go on through, I'm bringing the plates in now."

Soon they were all seated at the long dining room table digging into Shepherd's Pie. Senga was so famished she had polished off her helping before the rest of the family had barely started.

"Suffering cats, Lassie, you must have hollow legs," laughed Mr MacBean.

"Och, you leave her be now, Quin. She's a growing girl," laughed Mrs MacBean as she heaped more mince then, more potatoes onto Senga's plate.

"Jings, Senga," teased Bobby, "I haven't even finished putting salt and pepper on mine and you're on your second helping already."

Everyone laughed and proceeded to tuck into the delicious meal. Nobody said anything for a while. Senga was soaking in the deliciousness of being at this table with this family again. She had dreamed of it for so long. She just wanted time to stand still but she knew that wasn't possible. She had to convince Bobby that moving to Australia was the best decision for him and she hadn't much time.

Soon dessert was being served. Apple pie with lashings of creamy hot custard. Senga thought she'd died and gone to heaven. She couldn't remember when or if she'd ever eaten so much all at one time, but she didn't care. Mrs MacBean's cooking was out of this world! Now a big pot of tea was on the table along with a huge plate of shortbread. Senga wasn't sure she would like the tea but decided to try it. Jean poured some milk into her cup and added the hot liquid. Senga took a sip. She screwed up her nose.

"What's wrong? Do you need sugar," offered Bobby, passing her the bowl.

"Um, yes please," answered Senga, taking a couple of cubes and plopping them into her cup. She gave it a stir and took another sip. "Perfect!" She smiled at Bobby and he gave her a wink and a grin.

"Senga, did the girls tell you we'll be moving to Australia soon?" asked Mrs MacBean as she tried to coax her young visitor with one more piece of shortbread.

This was met by a loud groan from Bobby.

"Oh, Mum! Senga doesn't want to hear about all this moving stuff. Anyway, I'm still not going so that's that."

Senga looked uncomfortably at mother and son. A definite cloud had now settled over the family. Everyone was staring down at their plates not wishing to speak.

"Yes," responded Senga in a soft tone. "The girls were telling me. I think it's very exciting. I'm sure it will be hard to leave Scotland, but I've heard great things about Australia, although I've never been. What part?"

"New South Wales," responded Bobby in a grumpy voice. "Our uncle has a farm there and we're supposed to go out and stay with him until we get settled. We have to sell this place first though. Animals too. I'm just going to go live with my aunt and uncle in town and go to college. This lot can go by themselves and good luck to them!"

"Bobby, you don't mean that," wailed Mary. I don't want to go if you stay here!"

"Nor me," echoed Jean, her face crumpling with emotion. "Bobby, if you don't come with us, we'll never see you again. Australia is so far away. Our family has to stay together."

"Sounds like we've got a blooming mutiny on our hands," grumbled Mr MacBean. I'm tired of hearing you all squabble. We're ALL going and that's an end to it."

With that he jumped up from the table and stormed out into the kitchen. A second later the door slammed as he went outside.

Mrs MacBean looked as though she may start to cry. Senga felt so sorry for her, for the whole family. She could see that this decision to move was tearing them all apart. She had to do something, but what?

Chapter Twenty

The Conversation.

The girls had helped clean up after dinner then went outside to collect the ponies for the night. Senga was happy to be able to spend some time with the darling creatures. She buried her face in Dumpling's mane and stroked her velvety nose.

"All, right, let's get these wee beauties bedded down for the night." Jean announced. She threw halters around all three ponies and opened the gate. Senga suddenly stopped in her tracks.

"Wait, what's going to happen to the ponies if you're selling the farm?"

"They'll stay here, and the new owners will take care of them," answered Mary, wistfully. "It will be awfully hard to leave them though. We can't think about that at the moment. First things, first. What ARE we going to do with Bobby?"

"I have an idea," Senga answered slowly. "It's pretty drastic though, I'm going to have to tell Bobby the truth about me coming back from the future. He may totally freak out about the whole thing. What do you think, girls?"

Jean spoke first. "Why do you feel the need to tell him the truth, Senga? What good would it do?"

They were back at the stables now and getting the ponies settled in their stalls.

"Please trust me," Senga gave both girls a quick hug, "I promise I think what I'm about to tell him, and you both, will help you all with this move."

"OK, we trust you, answered Jean quietly, "and now's your chance because here comes Bobby. Hiya, brother, have you calmed down a wee bit?"

Bobby sauntered into the stable, hands stuck in the back pocket of his jeans, he smiled at all three girls.

"Yes, sorry I didn't mean to upset anyone tonight. It's just that, well, you know how I feel about moving to Australia. I just wish you'd all give over trying to convince me to go. Of course, I'll miss you all, but my mind is made up."

The three girls exchanged glances and Mary gave a nervous cough.

"Oh, what have you lot been cooking up?" Bobby laughed and walked over to Coal. Running his hand down the pony's broad back.

"Um, Bobby, can we please go somewhere and talk?" Senga took his arm and motioned for the girls to follow them out of the stable.

It was beginning to get dusk now.

"Let's go up to my room," suggested Jean
"OK," sighed Bobby, let's grab some chocolate biscuits and milk first."

A quick stopover in the kitchen for snacks and milk and the three headed up to Jean's room.

Bobby sprawled out on the floor in the corner of the room munching on the biscuits. Senga sat on an armchair next to him and both girls sat on the edge of Jean's bed.

There was dead silence for what seemed like an eternity and then finally Senga spoke. She started at the very beginning when she had first met Bobby, Jean and Mary in 1955, and didn't stop until she reached the part about her return several hours earlier. She felt drained and exhausted when she was done. She inhaled her entire glass of milk and sank back in the armchair half expecting Bobby to burst out laughing. She glanced over at the girls still sitting together, rigid on the edge of the bed. She then turned to face Bobby. He hadn't moved from his position either. He was staring at Senga in disbelief. Finally, he slowly raised both hands to his face and placed them on either side of his cheeks, his fingers covering his eyes. Senga was holding her breath waiting for him to say something… anything!

Chapter Twenty-One

Seeing is Believing.

Bobby cleared his throat and removed his hands from his face. His brilliant blue eyes were boring straight through Senga's.

"I'm not sure what to say," Senga. Bobby stood up and slowly started pacing up and down the room. He stopped and looked down at his sisters.

"Are you telling me you knew all this about Senga and kept it from me all these years?"

"Well,…" stammered Jean, "we only knew the part about Senga appearing from the future three years ago, then mysteriously disappearing again. We obviously didn't tell anyone else as we didn't think you'd believe us. I mean, do you even believe Senga? I know it sounds impossible and crazy and a million other adjectives that could describe what you have just heard. Mary and I have been stumped for the past three years wondering how Senga could just vanish from our field after falling off Dumpling. As astounding as it all sounds, this can be the only explanation. Senga is a time traveller!"

Now it was Senga's turn to speak again. She stood up from her chair and walked over to Bobby. She took his hand and turned his face towards hers.

"Bobby, there is one more part of my story that I must share with you. In fact, if I don't, the whole course of history could be changed. Please sit down again, this is going to take me a few minutes." Senga guided Bobby over to the chair where she had been sitting then knelt beside him. She relayed the recent Inverness trip to Bobby and the girls, every detail of her encounter with Weston, and seeing Bobby again. Senga concluded with the part where she had opened Weston's gift on the bus, then she reached over to her backpack and unzipped it. She pulled out the package and carefully unwrapped it. First, she held up the Nessie stone. Bobby took it from her and held it as though it were a precious, delicate flower. He stared at it intently then passed it over to his sisters. Next, Senga held up the photograph. If there had been any doubt in Bobby's mind that Senga had been making the stories up, he surely was now convinced that everything she had told them was 100% true. There could be no denying that he was now looking at a much older version of himself, his son and his grandson! Both girls were now crying and holding one another. Bobby finally put the photo down on the arm of the chair and looked at Senga.

"What an incredible gift you have, Lass! I'm sorry I doubted you, even for a minute. I should have known after meeting you three years ago that you wouldn't have been capable of making such things up."

Senga's eyes welled up. "Thank you, Bobby. I was so afraid to tell you in case you thought I was a whackadoodle.

"A whacka what???" Bobby laughed. "One of your new-fangled words, I'm guessing!"

Senga wiped her eyes with the back of her hand and giggled too but then her tone became serious again.

"So now you know why you HAVE to go to Australia with the family, Bobby, right!? If you don't so many people will die without that special Xray machine that you helped to invent. Plus, you all have had such a wonderful life out there. You won't regret it for a second."

"You have definitely convinced me, Senga. There is no doubt in my mind now that we will all be making the best decision for this family by emigrating to Australia. I admit, it will be very difficult to leave but it sounds as though I'll still be popping back to Scotland for visits."

The girls stood up from the bed and all four hugged tightly. Jean and Mary had begun to calm down a little. They both had been rather overcome with their emotions but hearing from Bobby that he would now be accompanying them had comforted them greatly.

Senga pulled away from the MacBeans and looked over at the clock on Jean's bedside table. She was shocked to see how late it was. She had to leave soon. Vespera would be waiting for her and Erdra had warned her to be on time.

Chapter Twenty-Two

Saying Goodbye.

Senga, Bobby and the girls went downstairs. Mr and Mrs MacBean were listening to the radio and reading in the living room. They both looked up expectantly as the four young ones entered.

"Mum and Dad," announced Jean, "Senga has to leave now. Bobby, Mary and I are going to walk her down to the end of the road where her dad will be picking her up."

"Och, that's a shame she can't stay longer. All right, Pet, it was lovely to see you again. Maybe you'll be back before we head over to Australia. I hope so anyway. You take care now, lovely Lass." Mrs MacBean jumped up and gave Senga a loud kiss on the cheek and a huge bear hug. Mr MacBean stood up slowly, stretching his back out and said quietly, "Cheerio the now, Senga."

"A man of few words is Dad," laughed Bobby.

Senga was glad of the little joke as she was trying desperately not to break down in front of the family. She quickly made a beeline towards the back door, calling out over her shoulder. "Bye bye, thank you very much for the lovely tea, it was wonderful to see you all again!" Senga bolted outside before she embarrassed herself and waited for the other three to follow her.

"You OK, Lass?" Jean put her arm around Senga as they started to walk toward the field where the Unicorn would be waiting to escort Senga back home. Senga gave a brave smile and nodded. She didn't trust herself to speak. In fact, none of them did as they trudged across the moonlit field. Soon they reached the edge of the woods and the stone wall where Vespera had dropped her passenger off. There was no sign of the magnificent animal. Senga instinctively knew why. She turned to her friends.

"You must all leave now, she said sadly. The Unicorn won't appear unless you do."

All three girls started crying again. Bobby too was desperately trying to keep a stiff upper lip, wiping his eyes with his sleeve.

"Senga, I don't know how we can possibly thank you enough," gulped Jean through her tears. "If it hadn't been for you, our family would have been divided and our lives never the same again."

Mary echoed her sister's thanks and then it was Bobby's turn.

"You're a brave, special, wee lassie, Senga. I've never met anyone like you, nor I expect ever will again. If I could change one thing it would be that I'd still remember you when we meet up again in the future." Bobby kissed her cheek gently and the three MacBean siblings turned and slowly began to walk away.

"I believe you did remember me, Bobby, I really do," whispered Senga to herself, tears now coursing down her cheeks. She kept watching them until it was too dark to make them out.

Suddenly she could hear hoof beats in the distance. She gave a sigh of relief. Soon the beautiful Vespera appeared in front of her. He pawed the ground and slowly moved his head up and down as though to greet her. Senga patted the side of his neck.

"Hello, Vespera, thank you for coming back for me."

She climbed up on top of the stone wall and he shifted closer to her. From there she could easily move onto his broad back, and clutching his thick mane made herself ready for her return journey. She laid her head down across his neck, she just realized how exhausted she was. She said a silent prayer that she'd end up back in Dunoon in the correct year!

Chapter Twenty-Three

Back to Reality.

Senga was amazed that she had slept the whole way back. Vespera was now walking slowly through the same woods where they had first met. She sat up straight and stretched her stiff arms and legs. She felt surprisingly rested. She had no clue how long she'd been asleep. She heard a melodic voice calling out to her. It was Erdra.

"Welcome home my little traveler!" The Selkie reached out her arms to help Senga dismount. "How are you? Was your trip everything you hoped it would be?"

"It was fantastic, Erdra. I know it was only twelve hours, but I feel as though I've been gone for weeks. I have so much to tell you."

Erdra smiled sweetly at her young friend. "I'm so happy to hear that! First let us say goodbye to Vespera. He can't stay around here too much longer. They both turned to the Unicorn and Senga stood on her tip toes to put her arms around his neck. "Thank you from the bottom of my heart, Vespera. I owe you so much for fulfilling my dream."

Erdra spoke to the animal in their strange language and also hugged him tightly. Vespera nodded several times then turned around and breaking into an immediate gallop, vanished from sight in an instant.

The two linked arms and proceeded to walk out of the woods and back down to the west bay where they'd originally met.

"I need to get home as quickly as possible," said Senga worriedly. "My aunt and uncle will be wondering where I am."

"Of course, sweet girl, of course. Look, there is the bus stop. You can be dropped off very close to your house. I think one should be arriving very soon." She kissed Senga on the forehead. "Please come see us at the shop before you head back to America. Would you?"

"Of course," responded Senga emotionally. She was so grateful for all that Erdra had done for her. They hugged and the next thing the bus appeared from around the corner.

"Great timing," Erdra laughed. Senga jumped on and waving goodbye to the selkie, sank back into a seat. Her mind was racing with everything that had happened the last twelve hours. She would have to have some answers for Tony as she would no doubt be bombarding her with questions about her 'sleepover' with Dasla. *Ugh, more white lies,* she thought. *I'm beginning to be an expert at this.* She hated it but what else could she do?

The bus finally arrived at the house. Senga walked up the driveway. She could see Tony's cheeky face at the window. She was waving wildly and grinning from ear to ear. *At least she's in a good mood,* thought Senga, smiling to herself.

Chapter Twenty-Four

Florida Bound.

Senga had slept pretty much round the clock upon returning from her escapade. Everyone assumed it was because she and Dasla had stayed up late talking at the 'sleepover.' Now the girls were having to pack as they were returning to the States the next day. As usual, Senga was neat and orderly, folding her clothes nicely in her suitcase. Tony's case looked like a bomb had gone off and she couldn't get it to close. Uncle Alex had to come to the rescue and soon the girls were all organized. They had one last place to go, into town to say goodbye to Dasla and Tarla. Aunt Rena gave them a lift, dropping them off just outside the girls' shop. They were both working as it was Saturday and looked thrilled to see the cousins when they came in.

"Ah, good timing," laughed Tarla, "I was about to take my coffee break. Anyone else?" Tony wrinkled up her nose.

"Coffee? no thanks, do you have any Irn Bru by chance?" She had become a huge fan of the sugary drink. Aunt Rena had made sure she'd got in a good supply for the girls visit. All four sat in the back of the shop enjoying chocolate biscuits and their drinks. Dasla was careful to protect Senga when the topic of the 'sleepover' came up. Tarla too. Both girls knew what Senga had just gone through with her journey back to visit the MacBean family.

The shop began to get busy, so the girls had to finish up their break and get back to work. All four said their goodbyes with massive hugs and 'see you next time!'

"Maybe you guys could come out to see us in Florida," said Tony hopefully.

"That would be amazing" the girls replied in unison, waving goodbye as the cousins left the shop.

The next morning, bright and early, they were headed to Glasgow airport again. Senga felt sad to be leaving but she was also looking forward to seeing her family and friends again. She wasn't sure when she'd be back, but she did know that she would make the effort as often as she possibly could. She had promised Weston that they'd stay in touch, and she could hardly wait to reach out again to him. It was like a dream come true that she'd been able to make that connection.

Soon the girls' plane was taking off. Senga had a window seat this time. She raised the shade and looked down at the brilliant green fields below. She could see the farms and animals dotted about the landscape. Suddenly, something caught her eye. She sat up straight in her seat and put her face up against the window. There it was! A sight to behold indeed. A beautiful, majestic creature galloping like the wind through the fields. Mane and tail flying. Senga smiled and watched until the plane climbed through the clouds. Leaning back in her seat she closed her eyes and fell asleep dreaming of Unicorns, Selkies, and the Mac Bean family.

Ten Fun Facts About Scotland

Inverness is referred to as the happiest place in Scotland.

In 1668 there was an entire battle fought over cheese!

If the Loch Ness Monster does exist, it is assumed to be like a plesiosaur – a dinosaur that was expected to be extinct over 65 million years ago.

Unicorns can supposedly purify water.

Glasgow used to be one of the largest cities in the world.

College is free in Scotland.

Scotland once had a baby queen.

Greyfriars Bobby was a Skye Terrier who spent 14 years guarding the grave of his owner.

Braveheart was actually the nickname of Robert the Bruce, not William Wallace.

The world-famous Tikka Masala was invented by a Pakastani chef in Glasgow in 1971.

The story and characters in these novels are fictitious. Several existing towns and public places are mentioned, but the characters involved are wholly imaginary.